Handling
Obesity

by Jill C. Wheeler

Content Consultant

Dr. Kendra Kattelmann
Distinguished Professor
Department Head
Health and Nutritional
Sciences Department
South Dakota State University

Handling
Health Challenges

Essential Library

An Imprint of Abdo Publishing
abdobooks.com

abdobooks.com

Published by Abdo Publishing, a division of ABDO, PO Box 398166, Minneapolis, Minnesota 55439. Copyright © 2022 by Abdo Consulting Group, Inc. International copyrights reserved in all countries. No part of this book may be reproduced in any form without written permission from the publisher. Essential Library™ is a trademark and logo of Abdo Publishing.

Printed in the United States of America, North Mankato, Minnesota.
052021
092021

THIS BOOK CONTAINS RECYCLED MATERIALS

Cover Photo: Shutterstock Images
Interior Photos: Creativa Images/Shutterstock Images, 4, 21; Vadym Petrochenko/iStockphoto, 8; Steve Cole Images/iStockphoto, 12; Seika Chujo/Shutterstock Images, 17; Roberto Michel/iStockphoto, 24; Shutterstock Images, 30, 34, 65, 70, 73; iStockphoto, 38, 40, 54, 93; Franky DeMeyer/iStockphoto, 44; Benedicte Desrus/Sipa Press/AP Images, 48; Monkey Business Images/Shutterstock Images, 57; Igor Alecsander/iStockphoto, 61; Zhang tao/Imaginechina/AP Images, 66; Kateryna Kon/Science Source, 76; Gilles Mingasson/Liaison/ Hulton Archive/Getty Images, 78; Anthony Harvey/Shutterstock/Rex Features, 84; Arthur Stock/Shutterstock Images, 86; Ljupco Smokovski/ Shutterstock Images, 88; ORNL/Science Source, 90; Jeffrey Isaac Greenberg 17+/Alamy, 99

Editor: Arnold Ringstad
Series Designer: Megan Ellis

Library of Congress Control Number: 2020948037

Publisher's Cataloging-in-Publication Data

Names: Wheeler, Jill C., author.
Title: Handling obesity / by Jill C. Wheeler
Description: Minneapolis, Minnesota : Abdo Publishing, 2022 | Series: Handling health challenges | Includes online resources and index.
Identifiers: ISBN 9781532194986 (lib. bdg.) | ISBN 9781098215293 (ebook)
Subjects: LCSH: Obesity--Juvenile literature. | Overweight persons-- Juvenile literature. | Obesity--Social aspects--Juvenile literature. | Body image--Social aspects--Juvenile literature. | Obesity-- Prevention--Juvenile literature. | Health--Juvenile literature
Classification: DDC 616.3--dc23

Contents

Living with Obesity

Jess took a deep breath, and with her hand on the doorknob, she began her daily mental inventory. She'd have a healthy salad for lunch. She'd fill her water bottle twice. She'd eat an apple for a snack. And she'd bring a change of clothes for going out that evening with her friends. She hoped no one would comment that she always wore the same outfit when they went out. She was glad to have found anything in her size that would be cute to wear to a club.

With her mental checklist finished, she turned the knob and stepped out of her apartment and into the hallway. She bypassed the elevator and began slowly to take the stairs five flights down to the ground level. Going down was so much easier than going up, and her doctor had recently told her again that it was good exercise to take the stairs. Yet even climbing

Dealing with the stigma of obesity can be stressful.

down, her heart was beating rapidly by the time she reached the final landing. She felt worse when she climbed up though, and the stairs made her knees hurt too. She rested a moment at the bottom, then gathered her courage and stepped out into the street.

The sidewalk was already filling with people on their way to work. Jess held her head up and walked as confidently as she could, looking straight ahead. As always, she focused on ignoring stares, laughs, and sometimes even snide comments from strangers. At the bus stop, she carefully assessed each arriving bus, hoping to find one that was emptier than the others. When all were full and she could wait no longer without being late for work, she climbed aboard a bus.

That bus, too, was standing room only. Jess's face flushed as she felt the eyes of the other passengers scan her up and down, then quickly look away. She shifted her purse and tote bag to get a better grip on the railing along the ceiling of the bus. She had to be ready if the bus started or stopped suddenly. It would be a disaster to lose her balance and bump into someone.

Jess managed to dig her phone out of her purse without losing her grip on the railing. She flipped

Shaming on Social Media

Social media provides fertile ground for attacking people with obesity. Researchers analyzed a four-hour window of comments on Twitter, looking for usage of the word *fat*. They found that more than 56 percent of messages including the word *fat* were negative, while 32 percent were neutral. Of the negative comments, the most common themes reflected were gluttonous at more than 48 percent, unattractive at 25 percent, and sedentary at nearly 14 percent.[1]

Internet personality and influencer Jaclyn Hill experienced such cyberbullying in fall 2019 after gaining 20 pounds (9 kg). "I don't even want to log onto social media recently because all I see is comments about looking fat," she posted.[2] Hill addressed the situation with honesty and a positive message about dealing with anxiety.

through her texts, laughing to herself at the messages about the upcoming evening. Next to her, she overhead two young women laughing out loud as they looked at their phones. "I can't believe how fat he is now," one said, holding up her screen for the other to see. "Oh my god," the other woman said. "There's no way he'll be in another superhero movie looking like that."

At last, the bus reached her stop, and Jess stepped off as quickly as she could. Once inside her office building, she could relax a little bit. The people here knew her, and she had friends there. She had just

Those experiencing obesity may also have joint pain, making it difficult to remain active.

reached her desk and started her computer when her friend Hannah stopped by. "You're still coming with us tonight, right?" she asked. Jess smiled. "I wouldn't miss it," she said.

Trending Heavier

Jess is a fictional character, yet her experiences with obesity reflect life for millions of people around the world today. Obesity, a complex disease involving an excess of body fat, has been increasing both within the United States and globally for many years.

Obesity rates among adults in the United States have
risen from less than 15 percent in the early 1960s
to nearly 40 percent in some states by 2018.[3] The
increase in obesity rates for children and young adults
has been even greater. In
the 1970s, roughly 5 percent
of US children age two to
19 were obese. By 2020, that
figure had risen to more
than 19 percent.[4]

> "When I stand up to do a presentation at work, I'm all too aware that people see my size first, not me."[6]
>
> —Mellisa, contributor to a BBC radio program about obesity

In late 2019, researchers
at Harvard University's
T. H. Chan School of
Public Health released the
results of a nationwide
study on obesity. The new study included a sobering
prediction. It said that about half of all adults in the
nation would be obese within ten years. In some
states, the research indicated, obesity rates would
border on 60 percent.[5]

The impact of obesity on those who suffer from it
is as complex as the disease itself. Obesity has been
linked to increased rates of heart disease, stroke,
type 2 diabetes, and certain types of cancers. These
associated health challenges are among the leading
causes of preventable premature death. In addition,

The Forecast for 2030

Harvard University researchers created a stir in late 2019 with the release of a study that predicted a significant jump in obesity rates in the United States by 2030. The prediction was based on the survey responses of some 6.2 million Americans from 1993 to 2016. The survey responses allowed researchers to study how the obesity rates of respondents related to the states in which they lived, their levels of income, and other demographic measures.

The results predicted that increases in obesity rates were most likely among women, non-Hispanic Black adults, and those with annual incomes below $50,000. The researchers also expressed concern that rising obesity among low-income adults throughout the United States could lead to added weight stigma for members of that population.

the social stigmas and common biases attached to obesity can lead to shame and guilt, social isolation, and discrimination at school and at the workplace.

Obesity also remains a highly stigmatized and personalized condition. According to Linda Bacon, a scientist specializing in weight-related research, it is virtually impossible for people to separate the condition of obesity from the person who is obese. Bacon says efforts to reduce obesity, which typically are framed in a message of better health, often lead to more shaming and discrimination against the people with obese bodies. "You cannot wage war on obesity without waging war on the people who live in those 'obese' bodies," Bacon says.[7]

Bacon and other advocates for people with obesity are working to achieve greater societal understanding, acceptance, and empathy for this complex chronic health challenge. At the same time, researchers in fields such as nutrition, exercise science, and mental health continue to gain new insights into the ongoing challenge of living with obesity.

Fat Phobia

As the number of people living with obesity rises, so does the fear of becoming fat. Each year, Americans spend more money trying to lose weight than they spend on video games and movies. Forty-five percent of adults say they are worried about their weight some or all of the time. Even girls as young as three say they worry about being fat.

For some, this fear leads to an eating disorder. Approximately 70 million people around the world have an eating disorder, such as anorexia nervosa or bulimia nervosa. People with anorexia dramatically reduce their calorie intake in order to lose weight. Those with bulimia engage in binge eating followed by purging, such as self-induced vomiting. Eating disorder experts credit the rise in these conditions to the body images promoted by culture and media. When people compare their own bodies to such images, they begin to perceive their bodies as deficient or wrong.

Chapter *Two*

What Is Obesity?

The World Health Organization (WHO) defines obesity as "abnormal or excessive fat accumulation that presents a risk to health."[1] This categorization is based on a person's weight-to-height ratio, also called body mass index (BMI). This measurement takes a person's body weight in kilograms divided by the square of that person's height in meters. For example, a person who weighs 150 pounds (68 kg) and is five feet, six inches (1.7 m) tall has a BMI of 24.2.

Doctors use a person's BMI as a rough measure to help determine whether that person is overweight. In adults, people with a BMI of 25–29.9 are considered to be overweight. People with a BMI of 30.0 and higher are considered obese. In addition, BMI can be used to diagnose underweight individuals. People with a BMI of 18.5 or lower are considered

Using weight to calculate BMI is one way to determine whether a person has obesity.

underweight, a condition which can likewise cause health issues.

BMI became a common tool for assessing obesity due to its simplicity. However, obesity is a complex disease, and many modern health professionals caution that BMI should be used as a guideline instead of a hard-and-fast rule. The same formula used for men is used for women, and it applies across people of all ages, even though levels of body fat typically vary among these groups. In addition, the measure of weight does not distinguish between muscle and fat. Athletes and others who have a lot of muscle, which is heavier than fat, may have a high BMI even though they do not have excessive fat.

> "There is an ill-defined threshold at which a person is labeled as being 'fat' or 'obese.' However, it is based on the 'I can't define it but I know it when I see it' concept."[2]
>
> —Dr. Frank Nuttall, endocrinologist

The Role of Genetics

In diagnosing obesity, most health professionals begin by calculating the BMI. They then gather more information to better determine what might

Why BMI?

The formula behind the body mass index was developed by Belgian mathematician Adolphe Quetelet in 1832. Quetelet created the formula to determine the size of a "normal" man. His work was used to help governments allocate resources, but it soon fell into obscurity.

By the early 1900s, insurance companies were beginning to see the connection between obesity and negative health outcomes. It was faster and easier for insurers to use a height-weight calculation to estimate the risk of a particular policyholder than it was to use more accurate methods, such as physical measures of a person's folds of skin and fat.

In 1972, obesity researcher Ancel Keys determined that among all the potential height-weight formulas, Quetelet's was the closest to accurately representing the actual body fat ratio of a test population that was also directly measured. Keys renamed the formula the body mass index. The National Institutes of Health began using the index to define obesity in 1985.

be causing the condition and how severe it might be. While obesity is generally considered a situation of someone taking in more calories than his or her body needs to function, there are many other factors that can influence that equation.

Genetic influences on obesity are tied to genes inherited from one's parents. These genes can affect the amount of fat one's body stores and where that fat is distributed. Genes also influence how efficiently a body converts food into energy. They can likewise affect a person's appetite and the rate at which he or she burns calories while exercising. Health professionals who work with obese patients report that obesity tends to run in families. It is believed that this is due not only to genetics but also to shared eating habits and other learned behaviors.

Behavioral Causes of Obesity

People with no genetic predisposition to obesity can still find themselves at risk due to certain behaviors and lifestyles. Both quantity and quality of food consumed play a significant role. Obesity is more common in people who tend to eat more fast food and sugary beverages and fewer fruits and vegetables. Portion sizes also play a role, with obese people frequently reporting consumption of larger portion sizes than people with a lower BMI.

"Apart from tobacco, there is perhaps no greater harm to the collective health in the U.S. than obesity."[3]

—Harvard T. H. Chan School of Public Health

How calories are consumed also makes a difference. Drinking calories in beverage form can lead to less of a feeling of fullness compared to when calories are

Most fast food is unhealthy and less nutritious than other food choices. Eating too much unhealthy fast food can result in weight gain.

eaten in foods. As a result, it is easy to drink large quantities of sodas and other sweetened drinks, as well as alcohol, without paying attention to calorie counts. Health professionals note that people often underreport the number of calories they drink as opposed to the calories they eat. This can make diagnosis and treatment of weight issues that much more difficult.

A person's level of activity also plays an important role in whether that person is challenged by obesity. The human body needs calories for energy, and if

Soda Taxes

Beverages with high sugar content, such as sodas and energy drinks, have been called out as contributors to rising obesity rates. In response, several cities have placed special taxes on these beverages to discourage consumption. The first to do so was Berkeley, California, which placed a one-cent tax per ounce of soda on all such purchases beginning in March 2015.

Years later, it remains uncertain whether this kind of tax changes consumption habits. Many cities with the taxes report reduced sales of these beverages. Yet public health experts caution that changes in actual health outcomes are not being measured. They say that food and beverage companies may ultimately be able to do the most good by developing and marketing more products with less or no sugar.

those calories are not burned through activity, they likely will be stored as fat. People with jobs that require them to sit for long periods of time are at higher risk of becoming obese. Research also has shown that people who spend a lot of time in front of a screen, such as on a computer, a mobile phone, or a tablet, also are at higher risk. In addition, lower activity levels have been shown to put people with physical disabilities at higher risk of obesity.

Metabolism, Hormones, and Aging

Metabolism and hormones also affect obesity. Metabolism refers to the chemical changes that happen inside the cells of living things to turn food into energy. Hormones are chemicals made by the body that affect the body's processes and psychology. Individuals who struggle with obesity throughout their lives may have one or both of these factors influencing their weight at any one time. Unlike genetics, metabolism and hormones can fluctuate over the course of a person's life.

It is common for people who have never struggled with obesity before to find themselves facing it as they get older. Metabolism tends to slow as humans age, meaning the body burns fewer calories at rest. Maintaining muscle requires more calories than maintaining fat, so as people lose muscle due to aging, their balance of calorie intake and activity can become misaligned. The same number of calories someone consumed at age 40 might be way too many when consumed at age 60. Hormonal changes due to aging also can change how and where fat is stored. Many women report more issues with abdominal fat after menopause, the point in life when

Obesity and Disability

Research is clear on the connection between staying active and maintaining a healthy weight. Some people have disabilities that prevent or limit physical activity. In many cases, this can mean a struggle with obesity.

Adults with a disability are more than 50 percent more likely to be obese than adults without a disability. When surveyed, nearly half of adults who reported they had problems walking or getting around were obese. About one-third of adults diagnosed with either a cognitive limitation or a visual limitation were found to be obese. Researchers identified multiple reasons for the situation, including medications, a lack of healthy food options, and physical limitations or constant pain that reduced the subjects' ability to exercise or participate in other activities.

they stop having monthly menstrual periods, due to the hormonal changes that accompany it.

Other health conditions also can play a role. Certain diseases, as well as common medications such as antidepressants and antidiabetic drugs, can cause weight gain. Losses in mobility due to arthritis or painful joints lead to a more sedentary lifestyle, which also increases the risk of weight gain.

Income, Environment, and Lifestyle

Many social and economic factors play a role in a person's risk of obesity. How much money people make and where they live can affect their diet.

These things can also contribute to whether they have an opportunity to be active or whether most of their life is sedentary.

Shopping for fresh fruits and vegetables can be time-consuming, especially in areas where they are not readily available.

Is Obesity a Disease?

In June 2013, the members of the American Medical Association's (AMA) House of Delegates voted that the organization would officially recognize obesity as a disease that required treatment and prevention efforts. Just a year before, the AMA's own Council on Science and Public Health found there was insufficient evidence to call obesity a disease. The classification of obesity as a disease remains controversial. Proponents of the classification cite the many factors beyond caloric intake that influence whether a person becomes obese. These include medical disorders, certain medications, and personal differences in metabolism.

Those who oppose a disease designation for obesity point to the difficulty in accurately measuring obesity. They also note that obesity does not always mean someone is in poor health, so a disease classification might not make sense. Finally, they point to the potential for added discrimination against people with obesity if it is considered a disease.

Some people might want to cook with vegetables but they do not know how, or they do not have a kitchen that is well equipped for cooking. Others live in so-called food deserts, places in urban areas where it is difficult or impossible to find fresh, healthful foods. Still others spend their time with other obese people and adopt the habits and behaviors that contribute to weight gain.

There are multiple lifestyle factors linked to obesity. Because smoking acts as an appetite suppressant, quitting smoking can lead to weight gain. Not getting enough sleep can be another contributor. If a person has made previous attempts to lose weight, her or his risk of obesity increases. Frequent diets and weight loss achievements can backfire and make the body feel that it is starving. This leads the body to slow metabolism even further, which makes it easier to regain the lost weight.

Mapping Obesity

Perhaps more than other health challenges, obesity rates correlate to particular geographies. In other words, clear patterns of obesity are visible on a map. In the United States, the most common method of mapping obesity is tied to the Behavioral Risk Factor Surveillance System (BRFSS). The BRFSS is an ongoing telephone survey of individuals across the United States that is conducted by the Centers for Disease Control and Prevention (CDC).

The BRFSS began in 1984 by gathering self-reported data on residents in 15 states. Over time, the program grew to include all 50 states, plus the District of Columbia and the US territories of Guam, Puerto Rico, and the US Virgin Islands. The BRFSS has become the largest continuously conducted health survey system in the world.

In many countries, the obesity rate is well above 20 percent.

Obesity around the World

The United States is not the only country where high obesity rates are creating negative health outcomes. In 2020, the World Population Review cited the Pacific island nation of Nauru as having the world's highest obesity rate, 61 percent. The same data indicated that the top ten nations globally with the highest obesity rates were all island nations in the Pacific region.

The Middle Eastern nation of Kuwait ranks number 11 on the list of highest obesity rates, with a national rate of 37.9 percent. The United States is number 12, followed by the Middle Eastern nations of Jordan, Saudi Arabia, Qatar, and Lebanon. The lowest obesity rate in the world in 2020 was Vietnam, where just over 2 percent of adults were classified as obese.[1]

Researchers working with the BRFSS record interviews with more than 400,000 people each year.

These survey results have enabled researchers to create state- and territory-based maps of obesity rates, as well as breakdowns of the data by age, education level, race, and ethnicity. The maps provide compelling evidence of the complexity of obesity and its interaction with a variety of factors. The maps also show that obesity as a health challenge tends to hit some populations more severely than others.

Overall Obesity Rates Vary by State

The 2018 BRFSS survey showed that nine states had overall adult obesity rates

Immigration and Obesity

Immigrants newly arrived to the United States often have lower obesity rates than their US-born counterparts. In addition, they frequently settle in neighborhoods where there are other individuals from their native countries or cultures. Research shows these concentrated neighborhoods may offer some initial protection against the growing prevalence of obesity in the United States. This is due to slower acculturation.

Acculturation is the process whereby an immigrant begins to adopt the language and customs of his or her new country as well as interact with the people born in that country. Acculturation leads to greater income and employment opportunities for immigrants. However, as immigrants to the United States adapt their traditional diets to the diets of their new country, their weight tends to increase as well. For most immigrants to the United States, the healthier bodies and lifestyles they brought with them upon their arrival disappear within ten to 15 years.

of more than 35 percent. These states were Alabama, Arkansas, Kentucky, Iowa, Louisiana, Mississippi, Missouri, North Dakota, and West Virginia. The lowest rate recorded was 23 percent, which was in Colorado. Between these two extremes, survey data showed that 31 states had rates exceeding 30 percent, and 48 states had rates exceeding 25 percent.[2]

Mapping state-by-state rates across the whole country reveals a pattern in which generally, states in the West and Northeast report lower rates of adult obesity than those in the Midwest and South. Obesity rates in the District of Columbia, Hawaii, and Alaska fit with those of the western United States. In the US territories of Guam and Puerto Rico, adult obesity rates were less than 30 percent and less than 35 percent, respectively. Rates in the US Virgin Islands also were below 35 percent.[3]

In addition to calculating an average statewide obesity rate, researchers also subdivided the data to determine rates based on age, education level, race, and ethnicity. This data analysis revealed additional patterns and clues to the many factors behind obesity. Researchers identified obesity rates above the state averages in certain groups.

Demographic Factors

Regardless of the US state in which a person lives, BRFSS figures show that people in some age groups have higher obesity rates than people in other age groups. The 2018 data points to obesity in 44.8 percent of adults age 40 to 59. Adults age 60 and over report slightly lower rates, at 42.8 percent. Adults age 20 to 39 reported the lowest rate among adults, at 40 percent.[4]

Education also was called out in the BRFSS results as a factor in obesity rates, though it was less significant than other factors. Generally, individuals with college degrees reported lower obesity rates than individuals with less education. However, that difference was not consistent across racial and ethnic groups. Asian women and men did not report a difference due to education levels, nor did Hispanic men.

Income levels also correlated with differences in obesity rates. However, these results were not always consistent, and they varied according to the person's gender. In men, researchers found that individuals in both the lowest and highest income groups were less likely to be classified as obese than men in the middle income group. One exception to this rule was found in the data involving non-Hispanic Black men, where obesity rates were found to be higher in the highest income group.

Obesity rates in women also showed two distinct patterns. For most races and ethnicities, obesity rates among women were lower in the highest income levels than they were in the low and middle

"We've penetrated every corner of the world with junk food."[5]

—Barry Popkin, food science researcher at the University of North Carolina Chapel Hill

Obesity varies widely across different demographics.

income levels. However, this pattern was not seen in non-Hispanic Black women, where the obesity rate was generally consistent across income levels.

Rural and Urban Obesity Rates

Studies also have addressed differences in obesity rates between rural and urban residents. In 2018, an article in the *Journal of the American Medical Association* reported on an analysis of 15 years of data from more than 10,000 adults around the

Food Deserts and Food Swamps

The correlation between obesity and geography has led to research into the impact of particular environments on obesity rates. Two environments that have been studied closely are food deserts and food swamps. Food deserts are defined as residential areas that have limited access to affordable and nutritious foods, such as fresh fruits and vegetables. Food swamps are defined as residential areas that have high availability of fast food and junk foods, which are typically high in calories but lower in nutrients. Both are more likely to be found in low-income neighborhoods.

Researchers found that easy access to fast food and junk foods was more of an indicator of high obesity rates than a lack of access to affordable and nutritious foods. They have encouraged cities to look at zoning regulations to restrict access to fast food while at the same time creating incentives for better access to more nutritious foods.

United States. Unlike the BRFSS data, this data included physical measurements of participants as well as survey data.

The study examined obesity rates for urban areas of more than one million residents, small urban areas with less than one million residents, and rural areas. Researchers found an obesity rate of about 38 percent for women living in large urban areas. The rate for women living in smaller urban areas was 42.5 percent, and the rate for women living in rural areas was 47.2 percent. The rates for men were

Diabetes

Diabetes is a chronic metabolic condition that impacts how a body processes food for use as energy. The sugar, or glucose, found in food is a key source of energy, and the body uses the hormone insulin to get that energy into cells. When insulin is not functioning the way it should, people can have too much sugar in their blood.

People living with obesity often face the challenge of type 2 diabetes. More than 90 percent of people with diabetes have type 2. Unlike with type 1, which scientists believe is caused by an immune system reaction, the common causes of type 2 diabetes include being overweight and inactive. Type 2 also can be reduced or even reversed through lifestyle and dietary changes.

Uncontrolled diabetes frequently leads to additional health complications. It is the leading cause of blindness and kidney failure. It also is a risk factor for heart disease and stroke.

31.8 percent in large urban areas, 42.4 percent in small urban areas, and 38.9 percent in rural areas.[6]

Obesity Rates by City

Within urban areas, other analyses have sought to find which cities have the highest rates of obesity and are thus at risk for more negative outcomes. A 2020 analysis of the 100 most populated US metro areas by personal finance website WalletHub looked at 19 weight-related indicators. These included data on health challenges such as diabetes and high cholesterol. The analysis also reviewed access to healthy food, activity levels of residents, access to parks or natural areas, health-care resources, and more.

The results of the analysis largely mirrored reports from the CDC. Cities with the highest risk of negative outcomes from weight tended to be in the South. These cities reported higher rates of diabetes, high blood pressure, and high cholesterol, and they had lower rates of fruit and vegetable consumption and physical activity. Cities reporting the lowest rates of diabetes, high blood pressure, and high cholesterol were dotted across the United States rather than concentrated in any one region. These cities were also more consistent in reporting more fruit and vegetable consumption and higher individual activity levels.

"People are snacking throughout the day. Snacking is the normal thing to do in the United States. In France, you never see anyone eating on a bus."[7]

—Zachary J. Ward, public health specialist at Harvard University

Childhood and Adolescent Obesity

While obesity rates have risen dramatically among adults, the situation with children and teenagers is perhaps even more of a concern to public health officials. The United States has one of the world's highest rates of childhood and adolescent obesity. Roughly one out of every five young people in the United States is living with obesity.[1] The earlier an individual is challenged with obesity, the earlier he or she can start to experience negative outcomes.

Children living with obesity face many of the same health challenges as their adult counterparts. These include high blood pressure, elevated cholesterol levels, and diabetes. Children with obesity also can experience liver scarring and damage, a higher risk

Teenagers with obesity not only suffer from health conditions due to their weight but may also experience bullying and victimization.

of bone fractures, and disrupted sleep due to sleep apnea. Sleep apnea is a condition in which a person temporarily stops breathing during sleep. Sleep apnea leaves people feeling tired during the day and reduces their ability to concentrate and learn.

There also are psychological and social costs of obesity in children and young adults. Research has indicated that children struggling with weight issues often have lower self-esteem than their peers, and they face more anxiety and depression. These issues are made worse by the teasing and bullying that these young people commonly face. The result can be emotional and behavioral disorders, and these people may act out in the classroom or withdraw socially.

Obesity Bullying

Teasing and bullying related to weight issues is commonplace in schools. Researchers surveyed a group of Connecticut teens about what kinds of bullying they saw at their school. At least 84 percent of the students surveyed said they had seen an overweight peer being teased, including teasing during physical activities. More than 65 percent of the respondents said they had observed overweight classmates being ignored, avoided, or excluded from social activities.[2] The students also reported instances of overweight peers being teased in the cafeteria or having rumors spread about them. Verbal abuse and physical harassment of overweight classmates also was common.

A Growing Problem

Obesity rates among teenagers climbed four times higher between 1980 and 2018. The 2017–2018 National Survey of Children's Health analyzed state-by-state data on young people between the ages of ten and 17. The lowest statewide obesity rate was 8.7 percent in Utah. The highest was 25.4 percent in Mississippi.[3] Nationally, the United States recorded an overall 15.3 percent obesity rate within this age group. For the youngest children evaluated, 2016 data from the CDC indicated a national obesity rate of 13.9 percent among kids ages two to five and 18.4 percent among kids ages six to 11.[4]

"Weight gained each summer accumulates year after year since children don't usually lose it when they return to school."[5]

—Andrew Rundle, Columbia University Center for Children's Environmental Health

As with adult obesity rates, researchers uncovered differences related to race, household income, and the education level of the head of the household in which the children lived. Obesity rates were higher among Hispanic (25.8 percent) and non-Hispanic

A poor diet can contribute to obesity.

Black youth (22 percent) than non-Hispanic white youth (14.1 percent). Obesity rates among young people ages two to 19 decreased as the education level of the head of their household increased. However, rates by household income varied. The obesity rate for young people in the lowest-income households was 18.9 percent, compared with 19.9 percent in the middle group and 10.9 percent in the highest of the income groups evaluated.[6]

Reducing Obesity with Federal Nutrition Programs

For many years, researchers have collected data that shows obesity in young people is closely tied to the amount of money their families have. The research found that young people from lower-income households are at greater risk of obesity. In 2010, researchers began tracking obesity rates in low-income households participating in a federal program that promotes healthy eating and nutrition education. In 2019, researchers reported that participating in the program reduced the average obesity rate among two- to four-year-olds in 41 states from 15.9 to 13.9 percent between 2010 and 2016.[7]

The most significant decrease in obesity rates was 3 percent, recorded in New Jersey, New Mexico, Utah, and Virginia. However, several states reported increases. West Virginia reported a 2.2 percent increase, while Alabama and North Carolina recorded increases of approximately 0.5 percent.[8]

Risk Factors

Many of the risk factors for obesity in adulthood are the same for children and teenagers. Diet plays a role, with increased risk for young people who regularly eat fast food, food from vending machines, and baked goods, or who often drink sugary beverages. All of these items tend to be high in calories.

Physical activity level likewise plays a significant role. The WHO recommends that children ages five to 17 spend at least 60 minutes per day in moderate to vigorous physical activity. However, regular surveys by the organization show that more than 80 percent of all 11- to 17-year-olds globally fail to meet that goal.[9] In addition, research indicates that children and teenagers are spending even more time on sedentary activities such as watching television or playing video games. The research found that children who watch television for more than three hours per day have a 65 percent higher chance of becoming obese than children who watch television for less than one hour per day. In addition, boys who spent less than seven hours a week watching

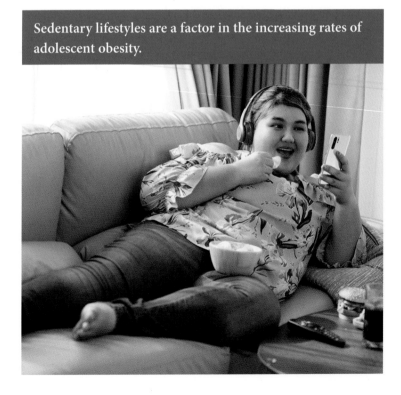

Sedentary lifestyles are a factor in the increasing rates of adolescent obesity.

television were 20 percent less likely to become obese adults than boys who spent more than 25 hours per week in front of a screen. The risk was 40 percent less among girls.[10]

Beyond diet and activity level, children and teenagers can face other risk factors for obesity related to their families, lifestyles, or environments. Researchers have identified that adults with obesity are more likely to be parenting children with obesity. This is due to members of the same family sharing not only genetics but also lifestyle elements, including more readily available high-calorie food and less emphasis on physical activities. In many instances, young people may be limited in both diet and physical activity by their economic circumstances. For example, they may live in neighborhoods that lack access to nutritious foods, or they may be in neighborhoods where it is unsafe to play outside.

Stress and other emotional challenges can play a role in youth obesity as well. A young person might grow up observing that family members deal with stress, sadness, or other emotions by eating and then adopt that habit as well. Boredom also can lead to overeating. In addition, young people who are living with obesity often find themselves in stressful situations because of how others, including family members, perceive them.

Gender and Ethnicity Impact

Research into childhood and adolescent obesity has uncovered some differences in obesity challenges among genders and ethnicities. Data from US government surveys in 2016 and 2017 indicates that nationally, nearly 16 percent of young people ages ten to 17 are living with obesity. Obesity rates vary by racial and ethnic background. The rate among Black youth was 22.5 percent compared with 12.5 percent for white youth. The rate for Hispanic youth was 20.6 percent, and Asian youth recorded a rate of 6.4 percent.[11]

"Childhood obesity isn't about looks. And it's not about weight. It's about how our kids feel."[12]

— Former First Lady Michelle Obama

However, these differences may be more related to household income than to race and ethnicity. Researchers looked at data of public school students within the state of Massachusetts. They found that obesity levels went down as household income increased, regardless of race. The study concluded

A Look Back at Let's Move

The challenge of childhood obesity had a high-profile advocate in former US First Lady Michelle Obama. Obama launched the Let's Move campaign in 2010 with the goal of solving the challenge of childhood obesity within a generation. In tandem with the campaign, President Barack Obama created the White House Task Force on Childhood Obesity.

The campaign and the task force resulted in healthier school meals and snacks, as well as more conversations around the need for physical activity for children and all members of the family. Multiple government agencies, as well as not-for-profit organizations and retail and food businesses, collaborated in the initiative. Obama tied the Let's Move campaign to new rules leading to clearer food labels. More prominent nutrition labeling has encouraged food companies to reduce sugar and fat levels in popular products.

that factors such as access to full-service grocery stores and access to parks and recreational activities played a bigger role in obesity rates than race or ethnicity.

Such research is important to public health and medical professionals in their work to better understand obesity challenges. Adolescents living with obesity have an elevated chance of being obese as adults. Interventions that reduce adolescent obesity rates can therefore be powerful tools in helping more adults improve their health outcomes as well.

Chapter Five

PETRO PAULO

RUBENS

CIVI OLIM SUO

S. P. Q. A.

SUMPTIB. PUBL. ET PRIV.

P.

MDCCCXXXX

The History of Fat Shaming

Shame is a feeling of failure and worthlessness. It is among the most painful emotions a person can experience. Shame is virtually a constant for many people living with obesity. Unlike many other health challenges, obesity is a challenge that everyone can see.

Dutch painter Peter Paul Rubens is perhaps the best known artist to feature subjects who would be considered obese by today's standards. The term *Rubenesque* has come to mean a full-figured, curvy woman. Rubens gained fame for his art in the 1600s, and fuller figures were admired up until the middle of the 1800s. Around 1600, there was a widespread belief that thinness of body equated to being poor, sick, old, and even morally deficient.

The Dutch painter Peter Paul Rubens is known for painting full-figured women, a body type that did not then have the negative stigma seen today.

Sara Baartman

In the 1700s, some white scientists attempted to find evidence to justify the enslavement and civil rights violations of Black people. Part of this justification included an analysis of body types, with the false premise that larger bodies were more primitive and therefore inferior.

This thinking is reflected in the story of Sara Baartman, an enslaved woman from South Africa who was publicly exhibited around Europe for nearly four years. The people who ran these exhibitions pointed to the large size of Baartman's buttocks and breasts as evidence of her lower level on the scale of civilization. Following her death, Baartman's body was quickly dissected, and parts of it remained on public display until the 1970s. Her remains finally received a formal burial in 2002.

These societal perceptions changed dramatically after the Industrial Revolution of 1760 to 1840. This period ushered in a time when more people lived in urban areas and fewer people lived and worked on farms. More jobs took place at desks, and they tended to involve less physical labor. These changes combined with improved access to food and more transportation options to create heavier bodies.

Popular media from the late 1800s and early 1900s indicates that public fat shaming was present in this time. Cartoons of the era featured obese characters portrayed as stupid or otherwise undeserving of the new wealth offered by a middle-class status.

Modern fat shaming likewise calls out people living with obesity as being weak, exhibiting a lack of willpower, and being lazy or sloppy. Some experts have referred to fat shaming as the last socially acceptable prejudice.

Body Size as an Indicator of Social Status

Research also shows a tie between a person's BMI and his or her status in society. Social status in this instance is evaluated by income and education levels. Researchers looked at BMI, gross national product, and socioeconomic status data from 67 countries. The data indicated that obesity levels increased as a country's economy developed. However, perceptions of the social status of people living with obesity changed as well.

> "Our culture assigns many meanings to fatness beyond the actual physical trait— that a person is gluttonous, or filling a deeply disturbed psychological need, or irresponsible and unable to control primitive urges."[1]
>
> —*Amy Erdman Farrell,*
> *Dickinson College*

In lower-income nations, people with high social status were more likely to be living with obesity.

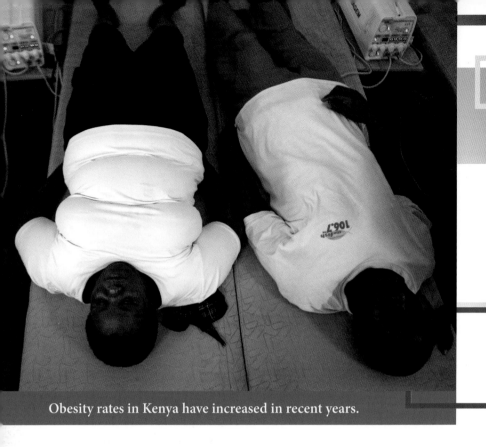
Obesity rates in Kenya have increased in recent years.

In high-income countries, individuals with higher social status were less likely to be living with obesity. Researchers theorized that higher-class residents of lower-income nations were able to consume more calories and avoid more physically demanding tasks due to their social status. In higher-income nations, higher-class individuals used the benefits of their social status to eat healthier foods and exercise.

Researchers also found that some nations demonstrate both scenarios. India, for example, is a very large developing nation. Growing incomes among many residents are leading to increased

Obesity in the Media

It's possible to see people living with obesity in movies and on television. Yet those portrayals are frequently unfavorable. Research on this subject goes back decades. Researchers evaluated body types in ten of the top-rated prime-time fictional television shows of 1999–2000. They discovered only 14 percent of female characters and 24 percent of male characters were overweight or obese. This was less than half the percentage found in the general population.[2] In addition, heavier characters were less likely to be considered attractive or to interact with romantic partners.

More recently, the NBC series *This Is Us*, which began in 2016, features a character, Kate, who openly addresses her relationship with food as well as family and love interests. Likewise, actress and comedian Melissa McCarthy has shown her box office appeal with movies such as *The Heat*. However, Hollywood still gives the vast majority of leading roles to individuals who are thinner than average. In addition, many plot lines continue to show overweight characters seeking to lose weight.

health challenges due to obesity rates. At the same time, many Indian residents continue to struggle with poverty and its corresponding challenge of malnutrition.

Education as a Key Element of Social Status

The complex relationship between social class and obesity continues to evolve as overall global obesity rates increase. For example, in the United States from

The Biggest Loser

Beginning in 2004, NBC aired *The Biggest Loser*, a reality television show offering prize money to the contestant who lost the most weight or highest percentage of body weight over the course of a season. The show, which has appeared in some form in more than 30 countries, has created significant controversy. Critics objected to the concepts of rapid weight loss programs and "fat camps," many of which fail to deliver long-term results. In addition, accusations were made that contestants were malnourished, dehydrated, or in some cases given weight loss drugs in order to lose as much weight as possible.

In 2017, the show went off the air. It was reborn under the same name on the cable channel USA beginning in 2020. The show's producers promised the 2020 season would introduce a new format focusing on a more holistic approach to wellness.

2011 to 2014, obesity rates among the lowest-income and middle-income tiers of adults were roughly the same at 40.8 percent and 39 percent, respectively. However, obesity rates differed based on education levels regardless of income. The same data showed the obesity rate of college graduates was under 28 percent compared to approximately 40 percent for the remainder of the population.[3]

Several theories have been proposed for why obesity levels in rich countries such as the United States are lower among individuals with higher levels of education. One theory is that higher education levels lead to different food and activity choices. Developed countries such as the United States feature a wide array of heavily marketed, highly appealing, high-calorie food options. These options also begin to appear in poorer countries as they develop, suggesting that a country's increasing wealth is tied to increasing obesity. More education may serve as a tool to help avoid overconsumption of such foods, just as a college degree has been shown to increase healthful behaviors such as using seat belts and not smoking.

Impact of Fat Shaming

Regardless of social class, income, or educational level, living with obesity involves living with fat shaming. In today's culture, fat shaming involves criticizing or harassing people about their weight or eating behavior. Often those doing the shaming are people who have never had to deal with weight issues themselves. They may think they are engaging in fat shaming as a way to motivate people to lose weight. Yet that is not what happens.

Research indicates that fat shaming is a common component of discussions about obesity, and this shaming is more frequently aimed at women. The research also indicates that fat shaming does not

The Social Invisibility of Obese People

Many things happen when people lose a large amount of weight. Some people have found that one of these things is becoming visible. "When I was obese, I was invisible," said Andy Kenny, who wrote about his experiences in the *Irish Times*. "People look past you—they don't acknowledge you. When I came home, I was slim and in shape and I noticed a difference in the way people treated me. They listened to what I had to say."[4]

Social invisibility is not limited to people living with obesity. People who use a wheelchair or who are elderly have reported similar experiences. However, individuals who experience weight loss often question why a different weight should make everything else about them different too.

lead to weight loss. Rather, it leads to increased stress that frequently increases caloric intake. In one study, women who watched a stigmatizing video ate three times as many calories afterwards as those who watched a non-stigmatizing video. A separate study found that weight discrimination more than doubled the odds of people not living with obesity becoming obese in subsequent years.

In 2013, blogger Melissa McEwan created a hashtag to call attention to the many ways people living with obesity are shamed each day. "I am constantly underestimated," was one response. "My intelligence, my strength, my talents, my tenacity, my cleanliness, my humanity." Another wrote of hearing that "Fat people are not disciplined enough to get a higher degree."[5] Still others wrote of being shamed for eating anything at all at a restaurant. Some said they had been told not to seek a particular job until after losing weight.

The public awareness of issues surrounding obesity, shame, and social status continues to evolve as more research takes place. One thing, however, is certain. Obesity remains a complex health challenge involving many genetic, environmental, and social factors.

"Media reporting tends to promote weight bias and focus the public primarily upon individual behaviors without addressing the complexity that leads to the current pandemic of obesity."[6]

—Fatima Cody Stanford, Zujaja Tauqeer, and Theodore K. Kyle, in their article "Media and Its Influence on Obesity"

Obesity Discrimination

In 2017, a group of researchers pored through existing studies that examined income levels and obesity rates. Many of these studies indicated that lower incomes were associated with a higher risk of living with obesity. The research team set out to determine whether it was lower incomes that caused obesity or obesity that caused the lower incomes. They found it tended toward the latter. While low incomes create conditions that increase obesity, there is also strong evidence that obesity creates the conditions for low income.

One explanation for this finding relates to obesity discrimination in the workplace. People living with obesity face discrimination at many levels as they navigate their careers. In comparison to people with lower BMIs, overweight and obese individuals earn

People facing obesity may deal with discrimination and other obstacles in their careers.

Obese Candidates Need Not Apply

In early 2015, a British legal firm polled 1,000 employers who were responsible for recruiting for their companies. The firm asked whether the respondents would interview an obese person as a candidate when filling a job opening. Nearly 45 percent of the respondents said they were less inclined to interview obese candidates.

When pressed for why, respondents provided a variety of reasons for this discrimination. "Obese workers are unable to play a full role in the business," said one respondent. "They wouldn't be able to do the job required," said another.[1] Other responses indicated a belief that obese people were lazy or that obese people did not care about themselves, so it was unlikely they would care about their employers' businesses.

lower wages. They also are less likely to be hired, recommended for new opportunities, promoted, and assigned to desirable job opportunities. They are subject to more derogatory jokes in the workplace, receive lower-quality training, and are more likely to face severe disciplinary decisions.

The wage penalty for obesity is most pronounced in women. A 2011 study found that heavy women earned $9,000 less per year than their peers of average weight. For very heavy women, the figure was $19,000 less per year. In contrast, thinner-than-average women earned $22,000 more per year than average-weight

People who are overweight often have to deal with untrue stereotypes. Others may incorrectly assume they are unfriendly and unmotivated.

women. Obesity wage penalties can begin quickly. Women have documented weight discrimination at just 13 pounds (6 kg) over their maximum healthy weight based on BMI tables.[2]

In addition to this economic toll, obesity discrimination in the workplace takes a psychological toll. Research indicates larger-bodied employees are more likely to be considered undisciplined, inactive, less friendly, and less likely to succeed than those in smaller bodies. Employees living with obesity may even begin to believe that they are responsible for those perceptions, and they may experience shame and guilt as a result.

Trying to Fit In

These findings are supported by the stories of people living with obesity. A pair of Dutch researchers engaged a group of women who self-identified as fat to talk about their experiences in the workplace. The researchers specifically wanted to find out what the women had to do differently at their jobs as a result of their body sizes. What researchers learned was surprising.

One respondent talked about giving tours of her workplace to a student group. "During the tour, I walked faster than my usual walking speed. I did not want to confirm the prejudice that fat people are lazy or slow," she said.[3] A respondent working in an academic setting wore a badge listing her credentials so that people would not assume she was a cleaner or other low-status worker.

Other respondents talked about how many workplaces failed to address the needs of employees living with obesity. Some had to special order uniforms because the standard offerings did not fit. Some scouted meeting and entertainment venues in advance so they could make plans to deal with flimsy chairs. Some avoided taking jobs that required them to fly in too-small airplane seats.

Discrimination in Health Care and Education

In addition to weight discrimination at work, people living with obesity report discrimination in health care and education. Research has determined that many health-care providers hold strong negative opinions and stereotypes about patients living with obesity. In addition, obese patients report that many health-care facilities are blind to their needs in everything from the absence of armless chairs to the availability of properly-sized blood pressure cuffs.

The Challenges of Traveling While Obese

With a few exceptions, the travel and hospitality industries remain designed for people not living with obesity. Airplane seats and bathrooms, airport metal detectors, and many public transportation vehicles can present particular challenges for heavier travelers.

Airline regulations require that all passengers be able to sit in a seat with the armrests down and the seat belt fastened. This requirement may result in passengers having to request a seat belt extender. Some airlines require that people living with obesity purchase two seats.

Obese patients commonly report seeing a physician for one thing, such as an earache, and instead being told to lose weight. In addition, research indicates health-care professionals spend less time with overweight patients and believe that those patients are less likely to follow recommendations. A study of physicians also found that many associated obesity with poor hygiene, hostility, and dishonesty.

This bias leads to more negative outcomes for patients living with obesity. Fat shaming at the doctor's office makes some patients more reluctant to seek care, increasing the risk for more serious conditions later on. In addition, doctors who are only concerned with weight may overlook or misdiagnose other serious conditions. The medical research community also reflects a bias, often excluding overweight patients from clinical studies. This can lead to inappropriate dosage recommendations for heavier patients.

"Every doctor I saw looked past me. They did not ask about my diet or exercise. Instead, my body spoke on my behalf, proof positive of my assumed irresponsibility and neglect."[4]

—*Anonymous contributor to Self.com*

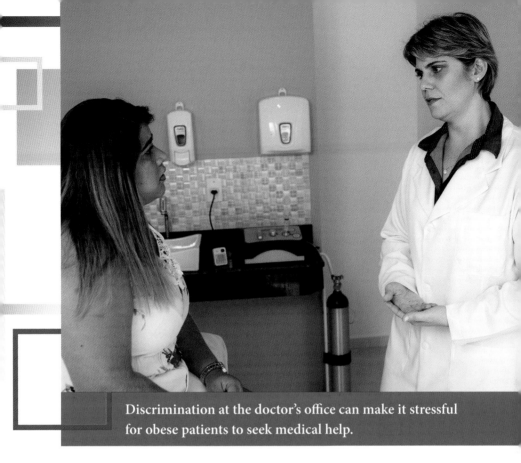

Discrimination at the doctor's office can make it stressful for obese patients to seek medical help.

People living with obesity also face special challenges in school environments. In addition to experiencing rampant bullying, overweight students are significantly less likely to be accepted to college despite having equivalent application rates and grades as their peers who are not overweight. This discrimination is even worse for women. One suggested reason for this was that overweight students received less financial support from their families than average-weight students. The researchers credited this finding to parental attitudes

Do You Have a Weight Bias?

Harvard University developed its Project Implicit tests to help individuals become more aware of the biases they hold. Since 1998, these tests have measured attitudes and beliefs that people may be unwilling or unable to report. In these tests, words are flashed on a screen and people must quickly categorize them.

Project Implicit includes a test dealing with body weight. Approximately three-quarters of the people who have taken the online test exhibit a bias toward thin people over obese people. In early 2019, Harvard reported that the test had recorded a drop in bias on the basis of sexual orientation and race between 2007 and 2016. Bias on the basis of weight, however, increased during that same time period.

emphasizing self-discipline, which lead to a bias against overweight family members.

As with health-care professionals, researchers believe many educators have a bias against overweight students due to misperceptions. This is due largely to the mistaken belief that a person's weight is solely under their individual control. Yet whatever the source, the outcome can create permanent damage. As one researcher stated, "Many fat kids exist on a diet of shame and self-hatred fed to them by their teachers."[5]

Seeking Legal Protection

Unlike discrimination based on race, age, disability, or sexuality, there are few if any legal protections against weight discrimination. Several New Jersey hotel employees sought legal action against their employer in 2008 due to the hotel's monitoring of their weight. The employees stated that the hotel would fire anyone whose weight increased more than seven percent from the time they were hired. The case went all the way to the New Jersey Supreme Court. However, the case was dismissed since there was no state law regarding weight discrimination.

"Obesity has been called the last socially acceptable form of prejudice, and persons with obesity are considered acceptable targets of stigma."[6]

–Dr. Scott Kahan, director of the National Center for Weight and Wellness

While support is growing slowly for anti–weight discrimination legislation, it faces an uphill battle. Employers argue that they need to be able to encourage weight loss among employees to control their health-care costs. Landlords express concern that renting to obese tenants leads to a need

The Obesity Double Standard

Some studies confirm women experience more obesity discrimination than men. Women experience a weight penalty at lower BMIs. Researchers have found that men report experiencing significant weight discrimination at a BMI of 35 or higher, while women report noticing discrimination at a BMI of just 27. This may help explain why women are significantly more likely than men to perceive weight discrimination in the workplace.

Obesity researchers attribute these differences to North American ideals of physical attractiveness. These ideals, which are promoted by the entertainment, diet, and fashion industries, emphasize being thin as a key element of attractiveness. This leads to stigma and discrimination even when women are only slightly overweight.

for additional repairs, modifications, and other costs. Opponents also fear an increase in lawsuits. Advocates say that fear is unwarranted. The state of Michigan has prohibited weight discrimination since 1976. In 2018, just 39 of the state's 2,100 discrimination complaints concerned weight.[7]

Weight-based discrimination is common in workplaces, health-care settings, and schools. This discrimination can have real and significant effects on those targeted, damaging their mental health, lowering their earning potential, and reducing

Discrimination can have a devastating effect on a person's self-esteem and mental health.

their quality of life. Advocates are pushing for an increase in awareness, along with strengthened legal protections, to counter discrimination and improve the lives of people living with obesity.

Causes and Prevention

The medical community has long told patients seeking to lose weight that they must reduce their caloric intake and increase their amount of exercise. Increasingly, research indicates that losing weight—and keeping it off—can be more complicated than that.

The reality television show *The Biggest Loser* provided researchers with an unusual pool of study subjects. Researchers tracked 14 of the 16 contestants on the show's eighth season in 2009 to see what happened to them following their dramatic weight losses. Six years later, 13 of the 14 contestants studied had regained their lost weight. Four of the contestants weighed more than when they began the show.

Researchers determined that the contestants' bodies had responded to their extreme weight loss

Adhering to an exercise and diet plan is crucial in preventing obesity, but obesity can also involve many other factors.

The Thriving Weight Loss Industry

Dieting fads have been a part of life for many decades. Low-carbohydrate diets have been around since the 1860s, and in the 1920s, people in the United States were encouraged to reach for a cigarette instead of a sweet. Popular diets in the 2010s included intermittent fasting and the keto diet.

Weight loss and dieting also can be big business. In early 2019, the United States weight loss industry was reported to be worth more than $72 billion.[1] The industry includes products and services such as diet sodas, artificial sweeteners, diet centers, health clubs, medical procedures to lose weight, and meal replacement products. Reports on the diet industry indicate that consumers may be reducing diet-related purchases as they seek healthier lifestyles versus just losing weight.

by lowering their resting metabolic rate (RMR). The RMR is the number of calories that the body burns in order to maintain basic functions such as breathing and circulation. Humans evolved this ability to reduce their RMRs in order to survive periods of famine. In today's world, however, this ability means that restricting calories too much can reduce metabolism in as little as two weeks. The body believes it is starving, and it reduces the RMR to conserve fat and energy.

Not surprisingly, the bodies of *The Biggest Loser* contestants had reduced their RMRs too. Yet one thing was different. Researchers expected the contestants' metabolic rates to slowly return to normal once the show ended. They did not. Even as many of the contestants regained their weight, their metabolism remained slow. On average, the contestants' bodies required 500 fewer calories each day than other people their same size. In addition, those who had lost the most weight on the show had the greatest change in RMR.

Unraveling a Multitude of Factors

Experiences such as these shed some light on why weight loss continues to be such a complex issue. Meanwhile, other studies are delving into why two individuals can go on the same highly controlled diet only to experience different outcomes. As one researcher described it, obesity, like cancer, is not one disease. It involves a multitude of

"Our bodies are evolutionarily programmed to put on fat to ride out famine and preserve the excess by slowing metabolism and, more important, provoking hunger. People who have slimmed down and then regain their weight don't lack willpower—their bodies are fighting them every inch of the way."[2]

—Madeline Drexler, editor at Harvard Public Health

factors beyond biology, including behavior, society, culture, and public policy.

To better understand these interwoven factors, some researchers have focused attention on individuals who have been successful in losing weight and keeping it off. A study of more than 4,700 people who had lost weight through a popular weight management program showed several common themes. Individuals who maintained their

Monitoring and scheduling regular activity can help with weight loss. It is also important to remember that progress is not always linear.

new weight reported more healthy dietary choices and more regular physical activity than those who did not. However, they also reported several other important behaviors.

One of those was weighing themselves at least once a week. Participants reported that this behavior allowed them to take action early if they began to gain weight. Those who maintained their weight also accepted that they would not always be perfect. If they ate too much, they would not criticize themselves and give up. Rather, they would make a plan to address what had happened and stay on track.

Another important difference for weight loss maintainers involved adopting specific health habits. These study participants reported that once they adopted certain habits, such as keeping low-calorie foods readily accessible, measuring portions, and tracking daily caloric intake, it became easier over time to maintain their weight loss.

Addressing the Environment

Another area of research into obesity involves how the proximity and availability of food impacts weight. Multiple studies indicate that people will eat more when they have the opportunity. A study by Google, which placed snacks in one of its offices either close to or farther away from a beverage station, found that people took more snacks when they were closer to the beverage station. Food columnist Tamar Haspel puts this kind of temptation another way: "Humans are simply ill-equipped to deal with a landscape of cheap, convenient, calorie-dense foods that have been specifically engineered to be irresistible."[3]

Other studies indicate that people exposed to tasty, calorie-dense processed foods naturally will eat more of those as opposed to unprocessed foods with a lower calorie density. One study divided people into two groups for 14 days. One group was given ultra-processed food items, and one was given unprocessed foods. Then, the groups switched to eat the other diet. Researchers found that both groups consumed about 500 more calories per day when given the ultra-processed food diet.[4]

Ultra-processed foods are foods that contain ingredients not generally used when cooking from scratch, such as artificial flavors, sweeteners, or preservatives. Examples of these foods include soft drinks, packaged snacks, chicken or fish nuggets, packaged baked goods, and instant noodles and soup. One study found that today, ultra-processed foods account for more than half of the calories that are consumed in America. These foods also are

Candy bars and snack foods have colorful wrappers that can be tempting for any consumer. Packaged snacks also have many processed ingredients.

increasingly prevalent around the world. Typically, these foods are high in calories, sugar, salt, and fat. They also tend to be cheaper and more readily available than unprocessed foods.

Researchers also are looking into how different labeling schemes can help people make more informed choices about what they eat. Nutrition labeling changes, along with food and calorie counting apps, have made it easier to see how many calories are in any particular meal or snack.

However, calorie numbers still may not mean much to most people.

To address that, researchers in the United Kingdom are testing a labeling system that equates the calories in a particular food to the physical activity that would be required to expend those calories. This is called the physical activity calorie equivalent (PACE). Under PACE labeling, for example, a candy bar labeled at 229 calories might also indicate that it would take the average person 42 minutes to walk off those calories, or 22 minutes to run them off.[5]

Initial results on the effectiveness of the PACE system are mixed. Some studies indicate PACE labeling led to smaller meals when people were exposed to that information. However, calorie counts alone do not provide nutritional information about how a particular food fits into a balanced diet. Critics of the plan also have expressed concern that it might lead to an increase in eating disorders and compulsive exercising.

Gut Check

One of the newest areas of obesity research involves the gut microbiome. The gut microbiome is the collection of microorganisms that live inside a

Bariatric Surgery

Bariatric surgery has become an increasingly popular weight loss and management option for people living with obesity. These surgical procedures are performed on the stomach or intestines. The objective of bariatric surgeries is to restrict the amount of food the stomach can hold and cause an imperfect absorption of nutrients by the small intestine.

Gastric bypass is the most commonly performed bariatric surgery technique. First, a small stomach pouch, holding approximately one ounce of volume, is created and separated from the rest of the stomach. Next, the upper small intestine is divided, with one part brought up to meet the newly created stomach pouch. The smaller stomach pouch allows for considerably smaller meals, and the divided small intestine has less opportunity to absorb calories and nutrients.

person's gastrointestinal tract. Each person has a unique gut microbiome.

A growing body of research indicates that the gut microbiome has an impact on many dimensions of human health, including weight. Scientists have found evidence that this microbiome influences how humans gain energy from their food, as well as how they use and store it. This has led researchers to believe that better understanding of the gut microbiome might lead to new tools to reduce or prevent obesity.

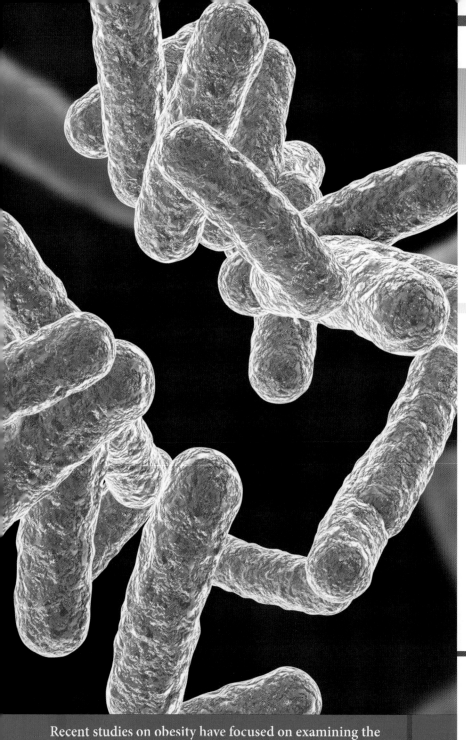

Recent studies on obesity have focused on examining the bacteria living in a person's stomach and intestines.

Studies already have found differences in the gut bacteria of children that could predict whether those children would become overweight. Other studies have found that lean mice gained weight when microorganisms from the guts of obese mice were transplanted into the guts of the lean animals. More studies need to be done to determine exactly what, if any, impact these microorganisms have on long-term weight management. Results also must be put in context of the many other environmental, socioeconomic, genetic, and behavioral factors that play a role in obesity.

"It would be great if there was a treatment that could come out of this research. But I don't think we're going to find some magic potion that will be able to cure obesity in the absence of any other intervention."[6]

—Dr. Elaine Yu, an endocrinologist at Massachusetts General Hospital in Boston, on research to treat obesity with microbiome transplants

FAT
is not a
four letter word

The Fat Acceptance Movement

On June 4, 1967, some 500 people gathered in New York City's Central Park to celebrate obesity. Like many similar gatherings in the 1960s, it was a protest. The "Fat In" was held to protest discrimination against overweight people. The event was organized by Steve Post, host of a local progressive radio program. "The advertising campaigns have attempted to make us feel guilty about our size," Post said. "People should be proud of being fat. We want to show we feel happy, not guilty."[1]

Later that year, US author Llewellyn Louderback published an essay in the *Saturday Evening Post* titled "More People Should Be Fat." Louderback said he was spurred to action because he was frustrated at seeing

For decades, people have been advocating for fat acceptance and body positivity.

Reclaiming the F Word

Part of the fat acceptance movement has involved a reclamation of the word *fat*. Once just an adjective related to the size of something, *fat* turned into a negative term in the 1800s as a large body size came to mean something other than a prosperous person. *Fat* as a derogatory term accelerated in the 1940s and 1950s as thinness became the societal ideal.

Today, more people living with obesity are using the term to describe their physical attributes. Their goal is for the word *fat* to become a neutral descriptor as opposed to an insult. Columnist Marie Southard Ospina writes, "My body is fat. I am fat. These are not insults. They're undeniable facts, and they don't negate my worth."[2]

how people discriminated against his wife, who was overweight. Louderback's article called out the stress and pain that fat discrimination in society imposed on overweight people. He also raised the point that much of the discrimination was not related to health at all but rather to aesthetics.

Louderback's article caught the attention of engineer Bill Fabrey. Fabrey was likewise frustrated by the weight discrimination his wife experienced. The two connected in 1968, and Fabrey went on to found the nonprofit National Association to Aid Fat Americans in 1969. Today, the group is known as the National Association to Advance Fat Acceptance (NAAFA).

These three events frequently are considered the beginning of the fat acceptance movement. Since that time, NAAFA and other groups have lobbied for anti–weight discrimination legislation. They have monitored fatphobic messaging in media and advertising messages and called out those who promoted such messaging. They have also held plus-size fashion shows, challenging the fashion industry to be more inclusive with its designs and sizes. And while all of these initiatives play out on a national scale, their most important contributions might be far more personal.

Your Body Is Not the Enemy

The fat acceptance movement began as a way to raise awareness of weight discrimination and the fat shaming that accompanies it. For people living with obesity, the movement also has become a call to stop treating their bodies as the enemy. "Fat acceptance to me is about learning to unpack the prejudices surrounding fatness that get drilled into our psyche from a tender age," says social media influencer and fat acceptance advocate Aarti Olivia Dubey. Adds another advocate, Maui Bigelow, "Fat acceptance activists empower fat individuals to love and express themselves despite their size and what others think."[3]

On a daily basis, the fat acceptance movement encourages people living with obesity to ignore messaging from society and media that says their bodies should look differently than they do. This can mean saying no to constant dieting.

"For more than half my life I struggled to not be fat," said Liz Black, who writes about fat acceptance on social media. "I started dieting in elementary school, did Weight Watchers, tried every fad diet out there . . . and yet I was still 'fat.' I fought so hard . . . to not look like what my body predisposed me to look like."[4] Whether due to fat acceptance or other factors, data indicates that fewer US adults living with obesity are trying to lose weight.

"Fat activism isn't about making people feel better about themselves. It's about not being denied your civil rights and not dying because a doctor misdiagnoses you."[5]

—Cat Pausé, researcher at Massey University, New Zealand

Fat Acceptance Misconceptions

The fat acceptance movement has helped many people living with obesity make peace with their

Healthy at Any Size

One message within fat acceptance is that an individual can be healthy at any size. In fact, the fat acceptance movement encourages people of all sizes to get out, be active, and participate in activities that bring them joy. Linda Bacon, author of *Health at Any Size*, clarifies that fat acceptance does not mean that everyone is healthy regardless of their weight. Rather, it emphasizes that everyone should switch their focus from their body size to how they take care of themselves.

This message includes people who are thin but physically unhealthy. A 2014 study showed that people who have average weights but high levels of body fat face challenges similar to people who are obese. Regardless of a person's weight, high levels of body fat increase a person's risk for cardiovascular disease.

bodies. It also has raised questions about how far acceptance of obesity can and should go. Some people have challenged that the movement is in fact promoting a condition that leads to many dangerous outcomes.

Former *The Biggest Loser* trainer Jillian Michaels made headlines in early 2020 when she was accused of publicly fat shaming musician and body image advocate Lizzo. Michaels later apologized for the remark but maintained that obesity had serious health ramifications. Fat acceptance advocates say such stories miss the point, however. Writer Rachelle

Hampton states, "If you've never been fat, it's hard to understand the various ways in which your body stops becoming your own once you reach a certain weight."[6] She notes how people living with obesity are subject to strangers giving them diet tips and evaluating their food choices, all in the name of being worried about their health.

Other controversies have arisen when body-positive role models lose weight and are

Rapper and singer Lizzo poses at the Brit Awards in 2020. Lizzo has often spoken about body positivity.

complimented on their new shape. Singer Adele lost more than 100 pounds (45 kg) after serving for years as an inspirational role model for fat acceptance. The new body earned her many compliments on social media, which some people interpreted as backhanded compliments. In essence, the positive comments on her new body implied that there was something wrong with her old one.

> "I am not pretty 'for a fat girl'—I'm pretty, period."[8]
>
> —D'Vaughn McCrae, writer

Ultimately, fat acceptance advocates say their movement is about ensuring that people living with obesity have equal rights and opportunities. "Fat people aren't trying to encourage more people to become fat," writes Hampton. "They're trying to live a life with dignity."[7]

The Body Positivity Movement

In 1996, fat acceptance took another step forward with the founding of an organization called The Body Positive by psychotherapist Elizabeth Scott and eating disorder survivor Connie Sobczak. The two set out to free individuals from negative societal expectations of body image that left them fighting with, rather than embracing, their own bodies.

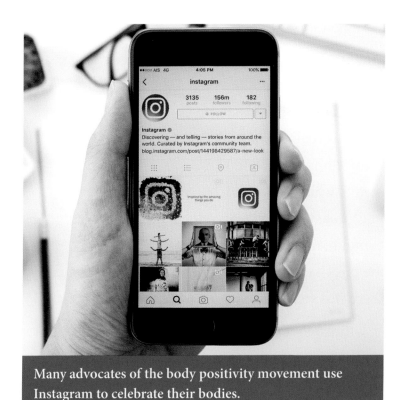

Many advocates of the body positivity movement use Instagram to celebrate their bodies.

The movement expanded and evolved, and by 2012, the focus had shifted from accepting fat to accepting that all bodies had value. Body positivity was spurred on by the rise of social media, in particular Instagram images, acknowledging a wide array of body shapes, colors, and sizes. A handful of consumer goods manufacturers also joined the movement, for the first time featuring unretouched photos of models or a wider variety of model bodies on product boxes.

BoPo Role Models

Social media has taken center stage in efforts to share body positive, or BoPo, images and stories. Plus-size models including Ashley Graham and Tess Holliday are among the millions of Instagram influencers who use the platform to promote acceptance of all bodies.

Increasingly, Instagram is proving a counterweight to the traditional fashion industry, which has been slow to embrace size diversity. While the platform still features images of six-pack abs and skinny-jeaned legs, it also has created an online community where people of all shapes and sizes are welcome to express themselves.

Instagram also has gained fans among organizations seeking to help people with eating disorders. These advocates say curating images of all kinds of bodies can be a powerful tool to help people see themselves in a more balanced, positive way.

The next evolution of body positivity is already helping to promote the acceptance of disabled bodies, as well as gay, queer, and transgender bodies. Similarly to people living with obesity, individuals in the disabled and LGBTQ communities often struggle with unrealistic expectations about what they should look like. Body positivity and acceptance can help them feel more at home in their own skin.

Chapter
Nine

A Bright Future

Doctors and researchers are learning more about common health challenges all the time. Obesity is no exception. More advanced understanding, new tools, and new technologies are all helping more people avoid obesity, overcome obesity, or create a healthier lifestyle while living with obesity.

Harnessing Genetic Differences

Researchers at Cambridge University in the United Kingdom analyzed the genetics of more than 500,000 volunteers. They discovered that about 6 percent of the volunteers had a gene that appeared to protect them from obesity.[1] The gene, called MCR4, appeared to affect how much a person ate.

Some individuals had a variant of the gene that seemed to suppress their appetites, leading them to eat less. Other research subjects had a different variant, which seemed to make them eat more.

Today, people with obesity are better able to live healthy lifestyles than ever before.

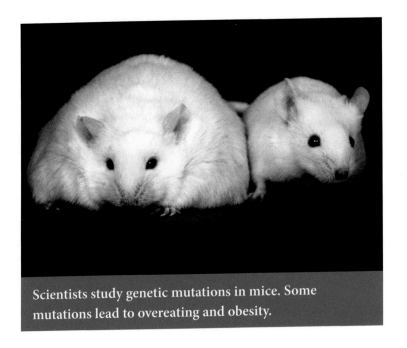

Scientists study genetic mutations in mice. Some mutations lead to overeating and obesity.

Subjects with two of the appetite-suppressing variants were found to weigh an average of 5.5 pounds (2.5 kg) less than people without these variants. In addition, they recorded a 50 percent lower risk of both type 2 diabetes and heart disease.[2] Researchers hope to use the results of the study to design anti-obesity drugs that help the body mimic the actions of the appetite-reducing genes.

Addressing Weight Bias in the Health-Care Community

Multiple studies have confirmed what many people living with obesity have experienced. Many health-care professionals have a bias against

Portion Sizes

Health professionals agree people in the United States are not trying to eat more, yet they are. Bigger portion sizes are one reason. The CDC reports that the average restaurant meal today is more than four times bigger than it was in the 1950s.

Another factor is how much people eat out versus cook at home. In 2015, people in the United States for the first time spent more on food prepared outside the home than on food prepared at home. Typically, meals from restaurants, including takeout, have more calories than meals made at home.

These facts, along with the increase in calorie-laden processed foods, have people taking in more calories daily. One estimate compared average calorie intake in 1970 versus average calorie intake in 2010. The difference was the equivalent of all people in the United States eating one extra steak sandwich every day.

overweight or obese patients. Increasingly, the medical community is taking steps to address this bias.

Several strategies have shown promising results in overcoming common biases against overweight patients. These include asking health-care providers to imagine if they were obese and how they would feel, or asking health-care professionals to test their bias through tools designed to detect unconscious biases. Other potential strategies include increasing medical training on nutrition issues, talking with medical students about the ethical considerations of this bias, and showing examples of the bias from popular media.

> "All diets work because they all address a different aspect of the disease. But none of them work for very long, because none of them address the totality of the disease. Without understanding the multifactorial nature of obesity—which is critical—we are doomed to an endless cycle of blame."[3]
>
> —*Dr. Jason Fung, nephrologist and weight management specialist*

Behavioral Insights for Weight Loss

As the counterproductive results of fat shaming become more widely known, weight loss advisers are choosing a different strategy. Initial results indicate people living with obesity can improve their health and well-being through a series of small changes designed to work with their existing lifestyle. This is the heart of long-term behavior change.

As an example, rather than forbidding someone from eating out at a restaurant, a modification might be for a person to still go to the restaurant but split an entrée with his or her dining partner.

For those with limited time for exercise, a small modification could be to walk the dog instead of letting it play in the yard. For those who dislike exercise altogether, they might start with just a short brisk walk, building up to three times per day.

This personalized, behavioral approach also addresses some key underlying causes of excess weight. Issues with stress management or lack of

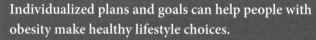
Individualized plans and goals can help people with obesity make healthy lifestyle choices.

Better Sleep for Better Health

Sleep is often overlooked as an important aspect of healthy lifestyles. Yet research shows that getting less than the recommended seven to nine hours of sleep per night may also play a role in obesity. Studies show that when people get too little sleep, they experience increased levels of the hunger hormone ghrelin and decreased amounts of the fullness hormone leptin. In addition, they consume about 300 more calories per day than their well-rested counterparts. Most of those extra calories are consumed in the form of high-fat foods. Sleep deprived people also are more prone to extra snacking from trying to stay awake and less physical activity due to feeling sluggish. Research suggests just five days of sleep deprivation can lead to weight gain.

sleep, for example, may seem unrelated. However, both have been found to contribute to weight gain.

Such modifications are unlikely to result in the dramatic weight losses of more extreme programs. However, these have been proven to be more long-lasting. Additionally, losing even a small bit of weight can pay off in better health outcomes. Research indicates even a slight loss in body weight in someone living with obesity can lead to improved blood sugar, lower blood pressure, and more energy.

Even the US military is adopting behavior change insights to address its growing challenge of rising obesity rates. Key to this effort is creating an environment where it is easy for soldiers to make healthful choices. This concept is known as choice architecture.

For example, the navy has eliminated fried food and sugary drinks on all of its ships. The US Marine Corps color-codes foods, with fruits, vegetables, and whole grains colored green. Fat-filled junk foods get a red label. Cafeterias feature salad bars and other healthy options at the front of the line. Higher-fat options are near the end. Military base convenience stores feature fruit and nutrition bars near the checkout instead of chips and candy bars. At the same time, bases are being redesigned to be more walking- and biking-friendly.

> "About eighty percent of the food on shelves of supermarkets today didn't exist 100 years ago."[4]
>
> —Dr. Larry McCleary, pediatric neurosurgeon

Inclusivity in Clothing and Fashion

Approximately 68 percent of all US women wear plus-size clothing, defined as size 14 and above. Yet a 2018 survey revealed that only 16 percent of online retailers' inventories went above a size 12.[5] Other retailers historically did not offer plus sizes at all, or they required that customers special order plus-size items at a higher price. That is changing.

In early 2018, women's clothing retailer Loft expanded its clothing line to include sizes up to 26. Notably, their larger offerings were the same styles and prices as their traditional offerings. Retail giant Target also doubled its offerings of plus-size fashion, rolling out the new items in stores beginning in 2018. Target also began expanding the diversity of mannequins featured in its stores. Size ranges for their mannequins now range from 4 to 22. Target and other stores are integrating the new offerings into their traditional store layouts as opposed to placing them in more remote areas of stores.

More diverse models also are making their way onto store websites, magazine covers, and even fashion runways. In March 2017, Ashley Graham became the first plus-size model to grace the cover of *Vogue* magazine. Also that year, fashion designer Christian Siriano included ten plus-size models in his New York Fashion Week show.

Gains such as these are small steps on the long road toward better understanding and acceptance of

Stress and Obesity

In 2017, researchers analyzed the connection between stress and obesity by studying levels of the hormone cortisol in hair samples of more than 2,500 people. Cortisol is the main hormone the body produces in times of stress. It plays a key role in managing how the body uses proteins, carbohydrates, and fats. Researchers found that the higher the level of cortisol in the hair sample, the greater the BMI, body weight, and waist circumference of the test subject. Unlike other studies of stress and weight, this analysis provided a more accurate indicator of ongoing, chronic stress.

Additional research has indicated that stress changes the quantity and types of foods that people consume. While people under acute stress may actually eat less, people under moderate to low stress are more likely to eat more energy-dense comfort foods that tend to be high in carbohydrates.

people living with obesity. Even as science strives to find answers and solutions to the health challenges of obesity, discrimination still exists against people with obesity. A study of ten- to 12-year-olds found that they harbored negative feelings toward overweight classmates even after learning about the many factors contributing to obesity.

Until society can catch up, advocates for people living with obesity encourage them to not apologize for their size. "When you pity someone, you think they're less effective, less competent, more hurt," says

Obesity and COVID-19

In March 2020, the World Health Organization declared COVID-19 a global pandemic. Medical professionals and researchers scrambled to identify this respiratory disease's patterns as confirmed cases and deaths escalated around the world. One pattern quickly emerged—COVID-19 patients living with obesity tended to experience the disease more severely, and die more frequently, than patients with lower BMIs.

Researchers at a New York hospital analyzed the cases of more than 3,600 COVID-19 patients. Patients under 60 normally were considered to be at lower risk for COVID-19 complications requiring hospital admission and critical care. However, the New York analysis found that even patients under 60 with a BMI of 30 to 34 were up to twice as likely to be admitted to the hospital for COVID-19 care than those with a BMI under 30 in the same age group.[7]

Patrick Corrigan, editor of the professional journal *Stigma and Health*. "The only way to get rid of stigma is from power."[6]

Obesity is a complex health challenge that affects millions of people in the United States and around the world. It is associated with not only physical health issues, such as diabetes and heart disease, but also mental health issues stemming from weight-based discrimination. Researchers and advocates are pushing for solutions to both sets of problems to improve the lives of those living with obesity.

Clothing stores have begun to increase representation of different bodies and carry a wider range of clothing sizes.

Essential
Facts

Facts about Obesity

- Obesity is a physical condition marked by excessive amounts of body fat that may lead to impaired health.
- More than one-third of US adults are obese, as are one in every five US children between the ages of two and 19.
- Obesity typically is measured by evaluating the ratio of a person's weight to her or his height using a formula called the body mass index (BMI). A person with a BMI of 30 or more is considered obese.
- Higher BMIs have been linked to increases in a range of conditions including type 2 diabetes, heart disease, stroke, and some cancers. Obesity also can lead to additional stress on joints, sleep apnea, and depression.

How Obesity Affects Daily Life

- Prejudice against people living with obesity remains widespread in most cultures around the world. This attitude results in discrimination, stigma, and shaming that adds to the negative emotional, economic, and health impacts of obesity.
- People living with obesity tend to earn less money, face more career limitations, receive a lower standard of health care, and be subjected to bullying and criticism at a higher rate than people of average weight.
- The fat acceptance and body positivity movements are helping bring more images of diverse body shapes into the cultural conversation.

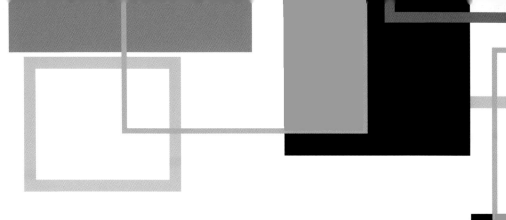

How Obesity Can Be Treated

- Obesity is a complex health condition marked by genetic, environmental, social, psychological, and economic factors. As such, it is difficult to address with any individual intervention.
- The most successful approaches for long-term weight loss and maintenance incorporate gradual but lasting changes in diet, activity levels, and behaviors. Drastic weight loss methods, such as intense dieting and physical activity, may lead to large weight loss in the short term, but these methods are not as successful over time.

Quote

"If you've never been fat, it's hard to understand the various ways in which your body stops becoming your own once you reach a certain weight."

—Journalist Rachelle Hampton

Glossary

acculturation
The process of a person becoming more like the people in the culture around them.

bias
Prejudice in favor of or against one thing, person, or group compared with another, usually in a way considered to be unfair.

calorie
A unit to measure how much energy or heat a food or drink can produce when consumed.

cholesterol
A waxy substance found in the body that is necessary for cell function. Excessive cholesterol can be damaging to health.

correlation
A close match between factors.

diabetes
A disease in which a person's body doesn't properly process sugar.

gene
A unit of hereditary information found in a chromosome.

metabolism

The physical and chemical means by which an organism processes energy.

pediatric

Related to medical care for infants, children, and adolescents.

processed food

Food that has been prepared with additional ingredients and packaged before being sold.

psychotherapist

An umbrella term covering medical professionals who are trained to help people with mental health problems.

shame

A feeling of guilt or disgrace.

stigma

A set of negative and often unfair beliefs that a society or group of people has about something.

stroke

A blockage of an artery supplying the brain or some part of it.

Additional
Resources

Selected Bibliography

Farrell, Amy. *Fat Shame : Stigma and the Fat Body in American Culture*. New York UP, 2011.

Fung, Jason. *The Obesity Code : Unlocking the Secrets of Weight Loss*. Greystone, 2016.

West, Lindy. *Shrill : Notes from a Loud Woman*. Quercus, 2017.

Further Readings

Carser, A. R. *Handling Diabetes*. Abdo, 2022.

Huddleston, Emma. *Nutrition and Exercise*. Abdo, 2021.

Snyder, Gail. *Kids and Obesity*. ReferencePoint, 2019.

Online Resources

To learn more about handling obesity, please visit **abdobooklinks.com** or scan this QR code. These links are routinely monitored and updated to provide the most current information available.

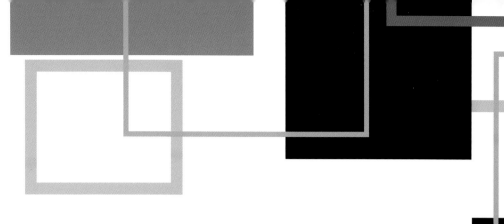

More Information

For more information on this subject, contact or visit the
following organizations:

Mayo Clinic

200 First St. SW
Rochester, MN 55905
mayoclinic.org
The Mayo Clinic is an American academic medical center
based in Rochester, Minnesota, focused on integrated clinical
practice, education, and research. The clinic features a variety
of resources to help diagnose, treat, and manage obesity and
the health challenges that accompany it.

US Centers for Disease Control and Prevention

1600 Clifton Rd. NE
Atlanta, GA 30329
800-232-4636
cdc.gov
The US Centers for Disease Control and Prevention collects and
publishes key health information, including the results of survey
data on obesity topics. The organization also encourages
public policies that make healthy eating and active living
accessible and affordable for everyone.

Source
Notes

CHAPTER 1. LIVING WITH OBESITY

1. Janet A. Lydecker et al. "Does This Tweet Make Me Look Fat?" *Eating and Weight Disorders – Studies on Anorexia, Bulimia and Obesity*, 11 Apr. 2016, link.springer.com. Accessed 19 Feb. 2020.

2. Neha Prakash. "Jaclyn Hill Responds." *Allure*, 10 Sept. 2019, allure.com. Accessed 19 Feb. 2020.

3. "Behavioral Risk Factor Surveillance System: 2018 Data." *CDC*, 9 Dec. 2019, cdc.gov. Accessed 27 Feb. 2020.

4. "Nearly One in Five US Kids Are Obese." *U.S. News*, 8 May 2020, usnews.com. Accessed 10 July 2020.

5. Nicole Rura. "Troubling Predictions." *Harvard Gazette*, 18 Dec. 2019, news.harvard.edu. Accessed 16 Feb. 2020.

6. "OK, I'm Fat – And This Is How It Feels." *BBC*, 13 May 2018, bbc.com. Accessed 11 May 2020.

7. Linda Bacon. "Fat Is Not the Problem." *Scientific American*, 8 July 2019, scientificamerican.com. Accessed 10 July 2020.

CHAPTER 2. WHAT IS OBESITY?

1. "Obesity." *WHO*, 2020, who.int. Accessed 10 July 2020.

2. Frank Q. Nuttall. "Body Mass Index." *Nutrition Today*, May 2015, ncbi.nlm.nih.gov. Accessed 23 Feb. 2020.

3. "Obesity Consequences." *Harvard*, 2020, hsph.harvard.edu. Accessed 12 May 2020.

CHAPTER 3. MAPPING OBESITY

1. "Obesity Rates by Country 2020." *World Population Review*, 2020, worldpopulationreview.com. Accessed 1 Mar. 2020.

2. "Adult Obesity Rates." *State of Childhood Obesity*, Sept. 2019, stateofchildhoodobesity.org. Accessed 29 Feb. 2020.

3. "Adult Obesity Rates."

4. "Overweight & Obesity: Adult Obesity Facts." *CDC*, 29 June 2020, cdc.gov. Accessed 10 July 2020.

5. Susan Brink. "Preconceived Notions about Urban vs. Rural Obesity." *NPR*, 8 May 2019, npr.org. Accessed 11 May 2020.

6. Nicholas Bakalar. "Obesity Rates Higher in Country than City." *NYT*, 21 June 2018, nytimes.com. Accessed 10 July 2020.

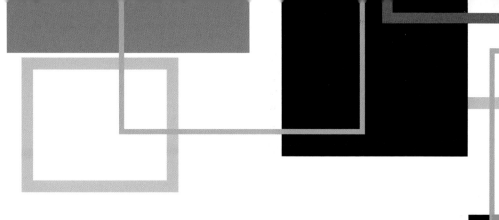

7. Jane E. Brody. "Half of Us Face Obesity." *NYT*, 10 Feb. 2020, nytimes.com. Accessed 10 July 2020.

CHAPTER 4. CHILDHOOD AND ADOLESCENT OBESITY

1. "Nearly One in Five US Kids Are Obese." *U.S. News*, 8 May 2020, usnews.com. Accessed 10 July 2020.

2. Rebecca M. Puhl et al. "Weight-Based Victimization." *JSH*, 4 Oct. 2011, onlinelibrary.wiley.com. Accessed 8 Mar. 2020.

3. "Obesity Rates & Trend Data." *State of Childhood Obesity*, 2019, stateofchildhoodobesity.com. Accessed 4 Mar. 2020.

4. "Overweight & Obesity: Childhood Obesity Facts." *CDC*, 24 June 2019, cdc.gov. Accessed 4 Mar. 2020.

5. Marlene Cimons. "US School Closings." *Independent*, 10 May 2020, independent.co.uk. Accessed 11 May 2020.

6. "Overweight & Obesity: Childhood Obesity Facts."

7. "Obesity Rates & Trend Data."

8. "Overweight & Obesity: Obesity Among WIC-Enrolled Young Children." *CDC*, 22 Nov. 2019, cdc.gov. Accessed 4 Mar. 2020.

9. "Drop in Children's Physical Activity." *Science Daily*, 11 Dec. 2019, sciencedaily.com. Accessed 7 Mar. 2020.

10. "Sedentary Behaviors and Youth." *Active Living Research*, Jan. 2014, activelivingresearch.org. Accessed 10 July 2020.

11. "Nearly One in Six Young People Nationwide Has Obesity." *RWJ Foundation*, 24 Oct. 2018, rwjf.org. Accessed 28 June 2020.

12. "Michelle Obama Interview." *Food Reference*, 9 Feb. 2010, foodreference.com. Accessed 10 July 2020.

CHAPTER 5. THE HISTORY OF FAT SHAMING

1. Amy Erdman Farrell. *Fat Shame*. New York UP, 2011. 6.

2. Bradley S. Greenberg et al. "Portrayals of Overweight Individuals." *American Journal of Public Health*, Aug. 2003, ncbi.nlm.nih.gov. Accessed 14 Mar. 2020.

3. Cynthia L. Ogden et al. "Prevalence of Obesity among Adults." *CDC*, 22 Dec. 2017, cdc.gov. Accessed 14 Mar. 2020.

4. Marese McDonagh. "When I Was Obese, I Was Invisible." *Irish Times*, 18 June 2013, irishtimes.com. Accessed 14 Mar. 2020.

Source Notes
Continued

5. Nina Bahadur. "14 Painful Examples of Fat-Shaming." *HuffPost*, 23 Jan. 2014, huffpost.com. Accessed 14 Mar. 2020.

6. Fatima Cody Stanford, Zujaja Tauqeer, and Theodore K. Kyle. "Media and Its Influence on Obesity." *Current Obesity Reports*, June 2018, ncbi.nlm.nih.gov. Accessed 10 July 2020.

CHAPTER 6. OBESITY DISCRIMINATION

1. Elizabeth Anderson. "Unlikely to Hire Overweight Workers." *Telegraph*, 9 Apr. 2015, telegraph.co.uk. Accessed 15 Mar. 2020.

2. Suzanne McGee. "For Women, Being 13 Pounds Overweight Means Losing $9,000 a Year in Salary." *Guardian*, 30 Oct. 2014, theguardian.com. Accessed 28 Mar. 2020.

3. Lila MacLellan. "The Treacherous Experience of Being 'Fat' at Work." *Quartz*, 9 Sept. 2019, qz.com. Accessed 29 July 2020.

4. "Weight Stigma Kept Me Out of Doctors' Offices for Almost a Decade." *SELF*, 26 June 2018, self.com. Accessed 15 Mar. 2020.

5. Rebecca Puhl and Kelly D. Brownell. "Bias, Discrimination, and Obesity." *Obesity Research*, 6 Sept. 2012, onlinelibrary.wiley.com. Accessed 15 Mar. 2020.

6. Jane E. Brody. "Fat Bias Starts Early." *NYT*, 21 Aug. 2017, nytimes.com. Accessed 11 May 2020.

7. Rebecca Puhl. "Weight Discrimination." *Washington Post*, 21 June 2019, washingtonpost.com. Accessed 15 Mar. 2020.

CHAPTER 7. CAUSES AND PREVENTION

1. "The $72 Billion Weight Loss & Diet Control Market." *Business Wire*, 25 Feb. 2019, businesswire.com. Accessed 22 Mar. 2020.

2. Madeline Drexler. "Obesity." *Harvard Public Health*, 2017, hsph.harvard.edu. Accessed 22 Mar. 2020.

3. Michael S. Williamson. "Connection between Poverty and Obesity." *Washington Post*, 20 July 2018, wapo.com. Accessed 10 July 2020.

4. Kevin D. Hall et al. "Ultra-Processed Diets." *Cell Press*, 2 July 2019, cell.com. Accessed 21 Mar. 2020.

5. Tim Newman. "New Food Labeling System." *Medical News*, 15 Dec. 2019, medicalnewstoday.com. Accessed 18 Mar. 2020.

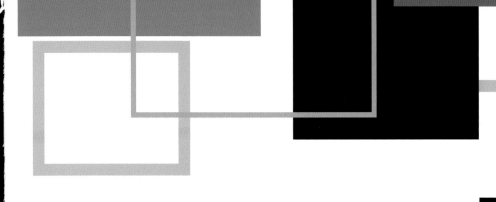

6. Anahad O'Connor. "Researchers Turn to the Gut Microbiome." *NYT*, 17 Sept. 2019, nyt.com. Accessed 10 July 2020.

CHAPTER 8. THE FAT ACCEPTANCE MOVEMENT

1. "Curves Have Their Day in Park." *NYT*, 5 June 1967, timesmachine.nytimes.com. Accessed 22 Mar. 2020.

2. Marie Southard Ospina. "I'm Done Treating the Word 'Fat' Like an Insult." *SELF*, 21 July 2017, self.com. Accessed 23 Mar. 2020.

3. Ashley Laderer. "The Fat Acceptance Movement." *Talkspace Voice*, 4 Dec. 2019, talkspace.com. Accessed 10 July 2020.

4. Laderer, "The Fat Acceptance Movement."

5. Michael Hobbes. "Everything You Know about Obesity." *HuffPo*, 19 Sept. 2018, huffpo.com. Accessed 28 Mar. 2020.

6. Rachelle Hampton. "The Fat Pride Movement Promotes Dignity." *Slate*, 11 Apr. 2018, slate.com. Accessed 22 Mar. 2020.

7. Evette Dionne. "Here's What Fat Acceptance Is – And Isn't." *Yes*, 24 June 2019, yesmagazine.org. Accessed 22 Mar. 2020.

8. D'Vaughn McCrae. "I'm Not Pretty 'For a Fat Girl'." *Yahoo Sports*, 15 Nov. 2016, sports.yahoo.com. Accessed 22 Mar. 2020.

CHAPTER 9. A BRIGHT FUTURE

1. "Genetic Variants that Protect against Obesity." *Science News*, 18 Apr. 2019, sciencedaily.com. Accessed 26 Mar. 2020.

2. "Genetic Variants that Protect against Obesity."

3. Jason Fung. *The Obesity Code*. Greystone, 2016. 217.

4. "Larry McCleary." *Goodreads*, 2020, goodreads.com. Accessed 11 May 2020.

5. Hilary George-Parkin. "The Price of Being Fat." *Teen Vogue*, 27 Aug. 2019, teenvogue.com. Accessed 28 Mar. 2020.

6. Michael Hobbes. "Everything You Know about Obesity." *HuffPo*, 19 Sept. 2018, huffpo.com. Accessed 28 Mar. 2020.

7. Stephanie Soucheray. "Obesity Appears to Raise COVID-19 Risk." *CIDRAP*, 10 Apr. 2020, cidrap.umn.edu. Accessed 26 Apr. 2020.

Index

About the
Author

Jill C. Wheeler

Jill C. Wheeler is the author of more than 300 nonfiction titles for young readers. Her interests include biographies along with the natural and behavioral sciences. She lives in Minneapolis, Minnesota, where she enjoys sailing, riding motorcycles, and reading.

About the Consultant
Dr. Kendra Kattelmann

Dr. Kendra Kattelmann is a registered dietitian, distinguished professor, and department head of the Health and Nutritional Sciences Department at South Dakota State University. Dr. Kattelmann maintains an active research program that focuses on prevention of excessive weight gain in young adults through healthful dietary choices and environmental support.